WALT DISNEY PRODUCTIONS
presents

Pete's Dragon

Book Club Edition
First American Edition. Copyright © 1980 by Walt Disney Productions.
All rights reserved under International and Pan-American Copyright Conventions.
Published in the United States by Random House, Inc., New York,
and simultaneously in Canada by Random House of Canada Limited, Toronto.
Originally published in Denmark as PETER OG DRAGEN ELLIOTT by Gutenberghus Bladene, Copenhagen.
ISBN: 0-394-83591-3 (trade)   ISBN: 0-394-93591-8 (lib. bdg.)
Manufactured in the United States of America   3 4 5 6 7 8 9 0   A B C D E F G H I J

Random House New York

Once upon a time there was a lonely little
boy named Pete.

Pete was an orphan.

He had no father or mother.

He had no sisters or brothers.

"What I need is a friend," Pete said
to himself.

Just then a large green dragon crawled
out of the bushes.
He had small pink wings and a big smile.
Pete was not afraid of him.
"Hello," said Pete. "Who are you?"

"Bippity, boppity," said the dragon happily. "My name is Elliot, and I want to be your friend."

Pete was very happy to have a friend
at last.

He skipped across the field with Elliot.

Then he jumped over a fence.

Elliot jumped over it too.

Later the two friends sat down
to rest.

Pete said, "I have run away from
the place where I was living. Now I
am on my way to see the world. Would
you like to come along, Elliot?"

"Bip, bip!" said Elliot. "Sure!"

Elliot knew that what Pete really
needed was a good home.

But he did not say that to Pete.

"I am hungry," said Pete. "But we have
nothing to eat."

"I will take care of that," said Elliot.

He wrapped his strong tail around
an apple tree and shook it.

Plop. Plop.

Bright red apples fell to the ground.

Pete wanted to roast some apples.

Elliot blew flames from his mouth to start a fire.

Then Pete put the apples on a stick and held it over the fire.

When the apples were cooked, Pete threw one to Elliot.

After their meal, the two friends started on their journey to see the world.

With Pete on his back, Elliot flapped his wings and flew up into the sky.

Soon it was late in the afternoon.

Pete and Elliot needed a place to spend the night.

They flew over a little town beside the sea.

"That looks like a nice town," said Pete. "Let us stay there for the night."

Elliot landed at the edge of the town.
Then he made himself invisible so that
he would not frighten anyone.

Pete and Elliot walked into town.
No one could see Elliot except Pete.

Elliot was a very large dragon.

By mistake he bumped into a man carrying fresh eggs.

Then he broke a wooden fence.

No one could understand what was happening.

A man who was fixing the sidewalk saw huge footprints in his fresh cement.

"What is going on here?" he shouted.

Pete and Elliot quickly walked out of the town and down to the beach.

There was plenty of room for Elliot
on the beach.
He and Pete went for a walk.

They came to some rocks on the beach.
There was a big cave in the middle
of the rocks.

"This is a good place to spend the night,"
said Pete.

Pete and Elliot made themselves at home
inside the cave.

They played tick-tack-toe together.

Once they even played it on Elliot's
stomach.

Suddenly they heard a friendly voice.
"Hello in there," it called.

The voice belonged to Nora, the daughter
of the lighthouse keeper.

She had heard voices inside the cave.

"Pete, go out and meet her," said Elliot.
"She sounds nice. I will be fine here
by myself."

Pete went out and shook hands
with Nora. "My name is Pete," he said.
"Would you like to meet my dragon?"

"I am sorry," said Nora gently, "but
I do not believe in dragons."

Elliot stayed hidden in the cave.
He wanted Nora to like Pete.

"You look a little tired and hungry,"
said Nora. "Would you like to come
home with me?"

Pete said that he would.

"Well, come on!" said Nora.

Pete and Nora walked off toward
the lighthouse together.

In the lighthouse, Pete ate a good dinner
with Nora and her father, Lampie.

Lampie was the lighthouse keeper.

Just as they finished dinner, a terrible
storm blew up.

Lightning flashed and thunder boomed.

"The light!" cried
Lampie. "It must
not go out!"

He ran up
the stairs
to the top
of the
lighthouse.

The storm grew stronger and stronger.
The wind howled.
Huge waves crashed against the rocks.

Not far from shore, a sailing ship was
being tossed about by the powerful waves.
But the light was still shining from
the lighthouse.
And the captain was able to steer his ship.

Suddenly the light went out.

"We are lost!" cried the captain. "Our ship will crash on the rocks!"

Lampie, Nora, and Pete were all at
the top of the lighthouse.

"Quick!" said Lampie. "Help me light
the lamp again."

Nora held the glass chimney.

Lampie tried to light the wick of
the big oil lamp.

But it was wet and would not catch fire.

Then Pete had an idea and raced down
the stairs of the lighthouse.

The wind and rain were very strong.
Pete ran as fast as he could.
He was going to find Elliot.

At last he reached the cave.

There was Elliot, sleeping peacefully.

"Wake up!" cried Pete. "You have to help
Nora and Lampie!"

In no time at all, Elliot and Pete were flying back toward the lighthouse.

Elliot was thinking so hard about reaching the lighthouse that he forgot to make himself invisible.

Nora was very surprised when she saw Elliot.

"Pete!" she said. "You really DO have a dragon!"

"Yes," said Pete, "and he is going to help us."

"Yee-ow!" cried Lampie. "That is a dragon!"
"Do not worry," said Pete. "Elliot is
a friendly dragon. He is here to help us."

Pete quickly showed Elliot the oil lamp
that would not light.

Elliot smiled and took a deep breath.

Then he blew out a strong flame.

The wick caught fire.
A bright light shone out to sea again.
"You did it, Elliot!" Pete shouted.

Then Pete and Elliot flew out over the ocean
to make sure there were no ships in trouble.

Soon Elliot brought Pete back to
the lighthouse.

Then Elliot returned to the beach.

The storm was over.

Nora fixed hot cocoa for everyone.

"Listen, Pete," said Lampie, "why don't you
and Elliot live with us? I could build Elliot
a special house on the beach."

Pete went down to the beach to tell
Elliot about Lampie's offer.

"Gee, Pete," said Elliot, "it is a nice idea.
But my work here is done. I came to you
because you needed a friend. Now that you
have Nora and Lampie, it is time for me
to go find another child who needs a friend."

Pete gave Elliot a big hug.

"You are the best friend a boy ever had," he said.

"Bip, bip, I know," said Elliot happily.

Then he flapped his wings and flew up
into the sky.

Pete and Nora and Lampie all waved good-bye.
Elliot knew that he would miss Pete.

But Elliot also knew that there was another
lonely child waiting for him somewhere. . . .